THIS WALKER BOOK BELONGS TO:

For Les, Cliff, John, Colin, Amanda
and the cats at Wood Green Animal Shelter.

First published 1994 by Walker Books Ltd
87 Vauxhall Walk, London SE11 5HJ

This edition published 2004

2 4 6 8 10 9 7 5 3 1

© 1994 Patricia Casey

The right of Patricia Casey to be identified as author/illustrator
of this work has been asserted by her in accordance
with the Copyright, Designs and Patents Act 1988

This book has been typeset in Bembo

Printed in China

British Library Cataloguing in Publication Data: a catalogue
record for this book is available from the British Library

ISBN 1-84428-786-6

www.walkerbooks.co.uk

WALKER BOOKS
AND SUBSIDIARIES
LONDON · BOSTON · SYDNEY · AUCKLAND

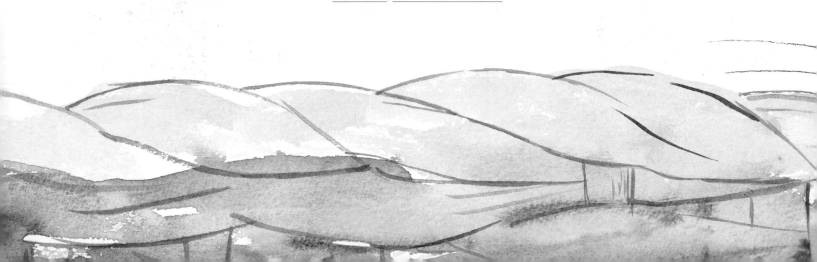

My Cat Jack

PATRICIA CASEY

My cat Jack is a

yawning cat.

He's a
stretching-down cat.

He's a
stretching-up cat.

My cat Jack is a scratching

cat.

He's a
curling cat.

He's a lapping

cat.

My cat Jack is
  a purring cat,
a rough-tongued cat,
  a washing cat.

He's a
cat who

likes washing
all over.

My cat Jack
  is a playing cat.

He's a pouncing

cat.

He's an
acrobat cat.

And sometimes
he's a silly old cat.
I love him,
my cat Jack.

WALKER BOOKS is the world's leading
independent publisher of children's books.
Working with the best authors and illustrators
we create books for all ages, from babies
to teenagers – books your child will
grow up with and always remember. So…

FOR THE BEST CHILDREN'S BOOKS,
LOOK FOR THE BEAR